Albert

Supersize

Ian Brown and Eoin Clarke

GRAFFEG

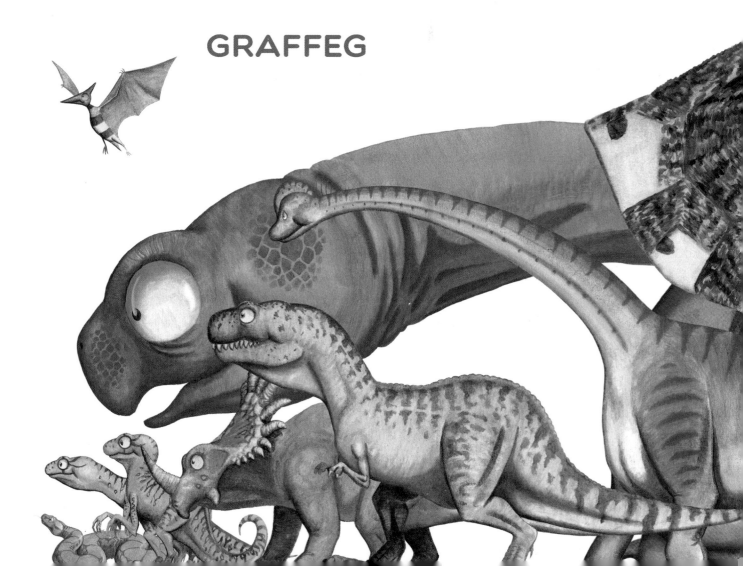

ROARR

This is a land of giant creatures
with mighty roars.

2

RRRRr

RRRrr

The biggest and loudest
of all is Albert.

At both ends.

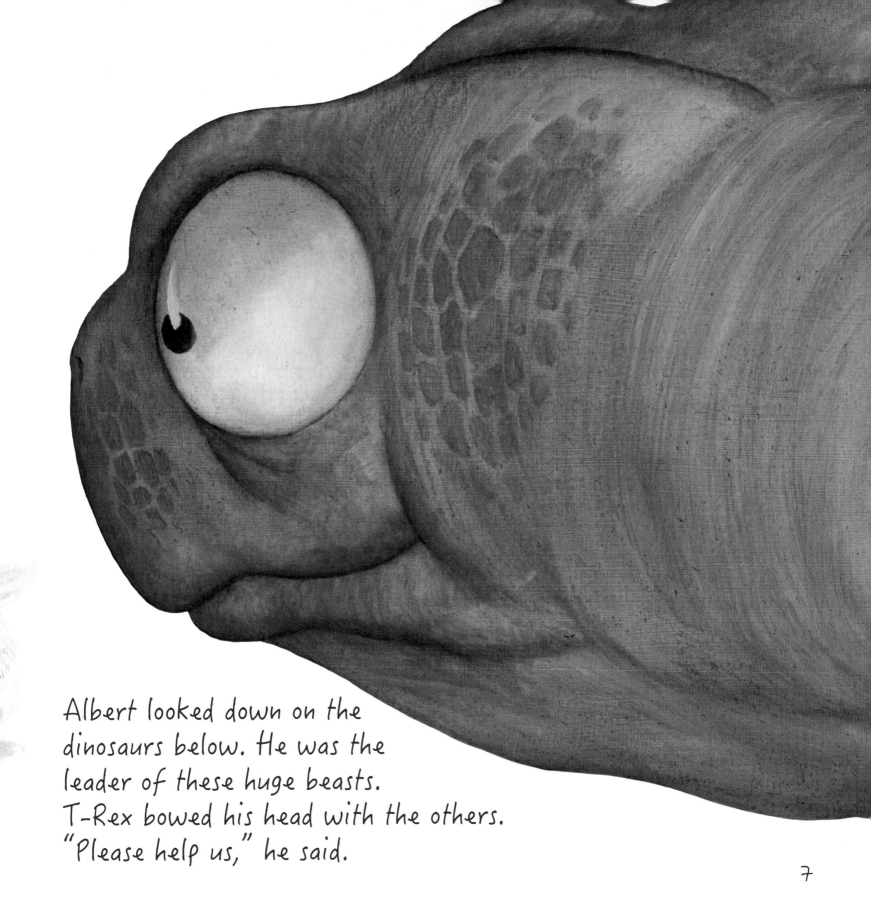

Albert looked down on the
dinosaurs below. He was the
leader of these huge beasts.
T-Rex bowed his head with the others.
"Please help us," he said.

The enormous volcano above their land was erupting.
Something had to be done.

With massive effort,
Albert shoved a gigantic
rock towards the summit.

11

It worked! The boulder snuffed out the volcano.

13

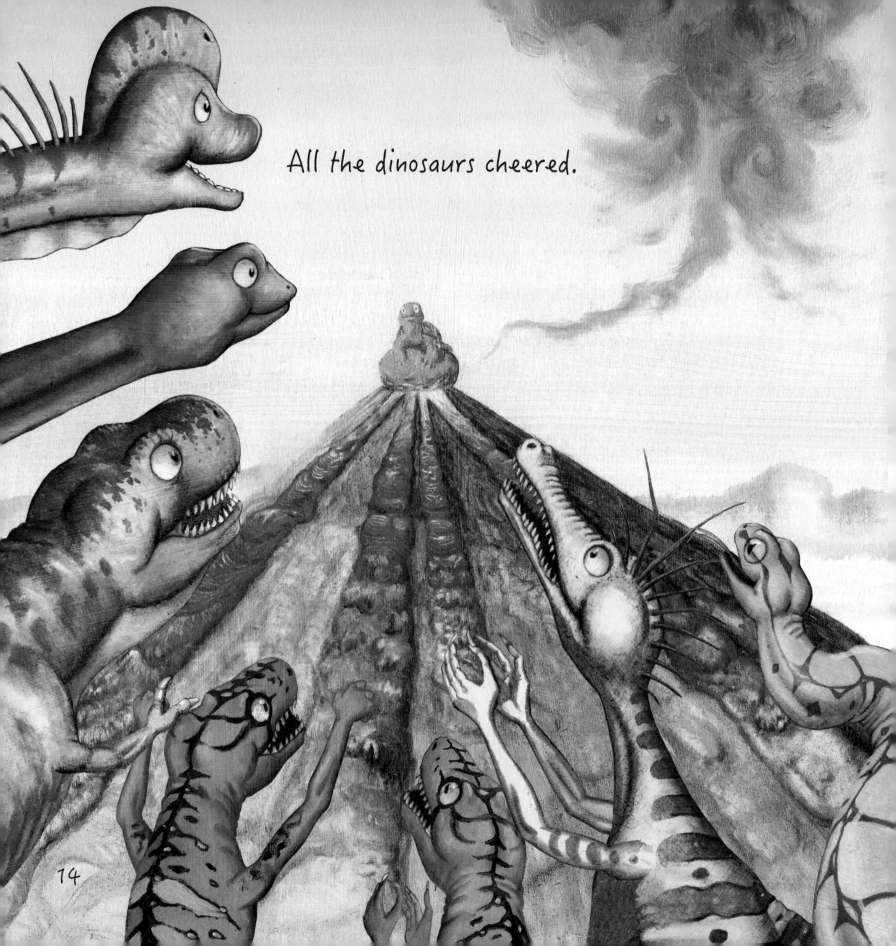

All the dinosaurs cheered.

14

Just as Albert was about to speak, the volcano shook beneath him.

15

Albert opened his eyes. His little
friends in the garden were shaking
him awake from his dream.

"I was a giant and
I was saving huge
animals,"
he explained.

79

"I always wondered what it might be like to be bigger," said Albert.

"You're already giant to us, and we need your help please," said a woodlouse.

22

"The flower pot we shelter under
has lost part of its roof."

"Now the light comes in.
We like the dark."

24

Albert studied the
situation. He had a
plan of his own.

26

Gently and carefully, Albert
pushed the rock back up the
side of the pot.

28

The little animals cheered as Albert
returned the rock to its position,
                covering the hole in the roof.

29

The ants were pleased
to be tidy again.

The woodlice were
happy to scurry back
to their home.

30

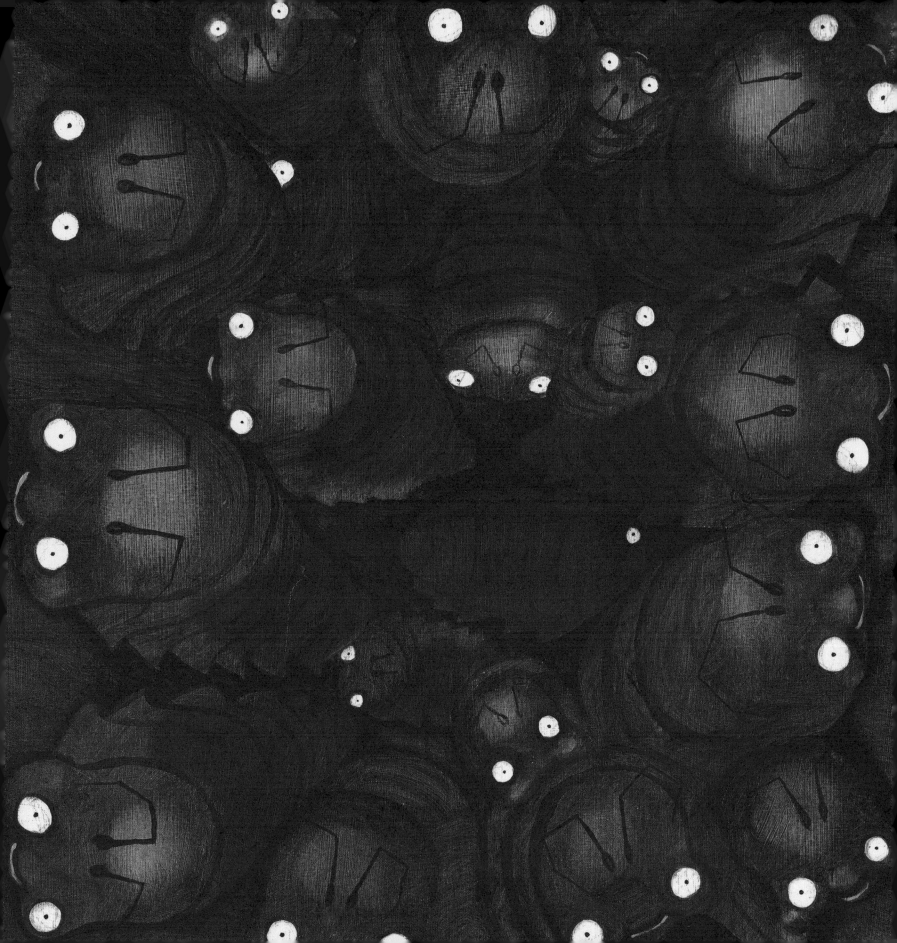

"You might have BIG dreams, Albert, but you're just the right size to help us," said a worm.
"I was going to say that," muttered an ant.

"Grrrr," roared Albert. Softly.

All the creatures laughed. No matter their size, they knew Albert would always be on their side.

Ian Brown

Ian is a former journalist, turned television writer and producer. After a spell on local and national newspapers, a thirty-year career in television has included news, documentaries, commercials, comedy and entertainment shows. He has written or produced for a host of household names, picking up several awards along the way. He's also often heard on radio talking about television. Writing for children has been a long-held dream. Ian shares his home with, among others, wife Millie, two cats and a tortoise called Albert.

Eoin Clarke

Eoin qualified with a BA in Graphic Design from Middlesex University and an MA in Animation from the Royal College of Art. He has worked for thirty years in the animation industry as a director, animator, designer and storyboard artist. He has directed films, commercials, documentaries and title sequences and has picked up thirty awards as a director, working on projects for, among others, the BBC, Channel 4 and the British Film Institute. Helping bring Albert to life has been a joy.

Albert

Albert, who inspired these adventures, was rescued more than 50 years ago by Ian's wife and her family. He has lived happily with the same family ever since. You can get to know real Albert better on facebook, @AlbertTheTortoise and on twitter, @AlbertTortoise and at AlbertTortoise.com.

Facts about Albert, tortoises and their dinosaur cousins

Albert in this story is based on a real tortoise – also called Albert – a modern-day, mini-dinosaur living life on the veg...

1. Real Albert is a Greek tortoise, also known as Mediterranean spur-thighed. Despite the name, they're also found in Northern Africa, Southern Europe and parts of the Middle East.

2. Real Albert spends his winters asleep in his special bed for around five months. This is one way some tortoises survive colder temperatures. He will also sleep at night through the months he is active. Some people use the term 'hibernation', but because he is a reptile, Albert's long winter sleep is also called brumation.

3. Studies suggest that reptiles like Albert might dream in some way when asleep, meaning that dinosaurs may have dreamt as well. You can do a lot of dreaming when you're asleep for five months.

4. Turtle cousins of Albert are among the most ancient creatures on Earth – they evolved before mammals, birds, crocodiles, snakes, lizards and even the dinosaurs themselves. The earliest turtles date from 250 million years ago. Tortoises date from around 55 million years ago.

5. It's thought that some dinosaurs had brightly coloured bodies and faces, and, like them, modern tortoises and turtles can have multi-coloured and patterned faces and shells.

6. One ancient cousin of Albert was called Megalochelys atlas. A true giant, it was the size of a small car and was the largest tortoise that ever lived. The shell alone could grow to 2.1 metres (6.9ft). The whole tortoise, counting head, legs and tail, could be more than 2.7 metres (8.9ft) long and weighed over 1 tonne. Fossils have been found in Asia (India, Pakistan and Indonesia).

7. These days, the largest living tortoises – also cousins of Albert – are the giant Galapagos, which live on the Galapagos Islands in the Pacific Ocean, about 965 km (600 miles) west of South America, and the Aldabra, which live on the islands of the Aldabra Atoll, about 730 km (454 miles) east of Africa. A Galapagos tortoise can grow longer than 1.3 metres (more than 4 feet). The Aldabra can weigh more than 250 kg (550 lbs).

8. Tortoises can live for a very long time. In 2021, when said to be 189 years-old, Jonathan, a Seychelles giant tortoise (related to the Aldabra tortoise), was hailed as the oldest known living tortoise and the oldest known living land animal. Originally from the Seychelles in the Indian Ocean, in 1882 he relocated to remote St. Helena in the South Atlantic.

9. The previous oldest tortoise was Tu'i Malila, a radiated tortoise, who reached 188 years old. She was owned by the royal family of Tonga.

10. Tortoises have been important creatures to humans for many years. In some parts of the world the tortoise is a symbol of wisdom and knowledge.

11. Always seek specialist advice before considering a tortoise as a pet and always consult expert guidance on tortoise care.

Books in the series

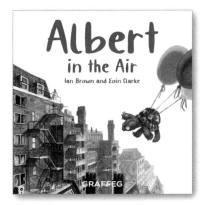

Albert Upside Down
ISBN 9781913634162

Albert the pet tortoise has a problem: trying to reach a tasty treat, he has ended up on his shell, upside down and stuck! Can the other garden creatures overcome their rivalry, team up and help him get back on his feet?

Albert and the Wind
ISBN 9781913733445

Pet tortoise Albert is having a bad day. His sleep is disturbed by the wind in the trees and then, as he goes to tuck into his food, the wind blows it away. Can the other garden creatures rally round and help Albert retrieve his meal? And will Albert be able to thank them all properly?

Albert Supersize
ISBN 9781802580167

Albert the pet tortoise is on his biggest adventure. He must tackle giant dinosaurs and a fiery volcano. Then, back in the garden, he's called on to help his little friends with a big problem of their own.

Albert in the Air
ISBN 9781802580174

A chance to explore takes Albert on an adventure he'll never forget, encountering first-hand the highs and lows of the world beyond. It's a journey of discovery that the grass isn't always greener on the other side... and that being home among friends is a very good place to be.

Albert digital books with narration and animation available from Apple iBooks. eBook editions also available from Amazon Kindle, Nook, eSentral, Google Play, Kobo and many others.

Albert Supersize
Published in Great Britain in 2022 by Graffeg Limited.

ISBN 9781802580167

Written by Ian Brown copyright © 2022. Illustrated by Eoin Clarke copyright © 2022. Designed and produced by Graffeg Limited copyright © 2022.

Graffeg Limited, 15 Neptune Court, Vanguard Way, Cardiff CF24 5PJ, Wales, UK. Tel: +44(0)1554 824000. www.graffeg.com.

Ian Brown is hereby identified as the author of this work in accordance with section 77 of the Copyrights, Designs and Patents Act 1988. Albert the Tortoise is a ® Registered Trademark.

A CIP Catalogue record for this book is available from the British Library.

Free to download Teaching Notes and Colouring Sheets.

1 2 3 4 5 6 7 8 9

MIX
Paper from responsible sources
FSC
www.fsc.org
FSC® C014138